MW01077155

Christmas Tree Farm

by ANN PURMELL

illustrated by JILL WEBER

Holiday House / New York

The illustrator would like to send special thanks to Mr. Pierce for his time and generosity, and for the wonderfully inspiring tour of Pierce's Christmas Tree Farm in Lunenburg, Massachusetts.

Manufactured in China
The text typeface is Steam.
The artwork was created with gouache, acrylics,
and collage on Strathmore paper.
www.holidayhouse.com
First Edition
1 3 5 7 9 10 8 6 4 2

Library of Congress Cataloging-in-Publication Data
Purmell, Ann.
Christmas tree farm / by Ann Purmell ; illustrated by Jill Weber.— 1st ed.
p. cm.
Summary: A boy describes how he, his grandfather, and the rest of his family
work on their tree farm throughout the year to prepare Christmas trees.
ISBN 0-8234-1886-3 (hardcover)
[1. Christmas trees—Fiction. 2. Tree farms—Fiction. 3. Grandfathers—Fiction.
4. Christmas—Fiction.] I. Weber, Jill, ill. II. Title.
PZ7.P977Ch 2006
[E]—dc22
2004047502
ISBN-13: 978-0-8234-1886-2
ISBN-10: 0-8234-1886-3

To my agent, Scott Treimel,
for his dedication and friendship
A. P.

For Charlotte

J. W.

Grandpa and I sit on the seat of his tractor. We drive along the path that winds through woods filled with Christmas trees. There are spruces, pines, and firs. Some of these trees are older than Grandpa.

It is November and snow sprinkles the ground. The air is cold. It nips my nose. We wear warm coats, hats, gloves, and boots.

Grandpa points to a tree with bushy branches. We climb down. "This is a good Scotch pine," he says.

Grandpa and I pull safety glasses over our eyes. The chain saw starts with a roar. Grandpa holds the whirring blade to the bottom of the tree, cutting through the trunk. Wood chips fly and the tree topples over.

Grandpa switches off the saw. It is quiet except for the cawing of crows. He holds the pine by its trunk and he shakes it. Dry needles fall to the ground.

Grandpa drags the tree to the wagon behind the tractor. "One, two, three." We lift the tree together into the wagon.

Back on the tractor, Grandpa nods at a Douglas fir with short, soft needles. We add it to our load.

We cut trees all afternoon. My gloves are sticky with pinesap, and the smell tickles my nose. By dinnertime the wagon is full of trees for people who cannot cut their own.

The day after Thanksgiving, Grandpa unlocks the door to the Tree Hut, where customers pay for their Christmas trees. He switches on the lights strung across the fence by the road. The Christmas Tree Farm is open for the holidays!

TREE HUT
CUT TREES
OPEN

Most people tramp through the woods until they find a Christmas tree that looks just right to them.

They cut down that tree and carry it to the Tree Hut, where we collect their money and offer them Christmas cookies baked by Grandma.

Keep Your tree in a cool place until it
comes in Shake it so the dead
needles fall off Cut off a
thin slice of the trunk so it
will get lots to drink Put
it in the stand and make
sure it always has
lots of water

People drive from everywhere to buy their Christmas trees from Grandpa. He loves to talk about the trees. He gives tips on how to keep them fresh at home. Grandpa talks as he pulls each tree through the baler. The tree comes out the other end covered with a net that holds the branches close to the trunk. Now it's easier to tie it to the roof of the car.

Most people do not know Christmas tree farming is yearlong work. . . .

In the spring, a truck delivers hundreds of seedlings that are not much bigger than Grandpa's hand. The seedlings have many enemies. There are insects and diseases, rabbits and deer. We lose many seedlings, so we must plant more than will ever grow into trees.

Grandpa, Dad, my sister, Emily, and I
plant the seedlings in straight rows.

Each row is about
six feet from the next.
We leave enough space
so we can drive a tractor
with back~end blades
between the rows, turning
up the soil so weeds do not
hurt the young trees.

By summertime, the trees are wild and shaggy with new growth. Under the hot sun, we trim and prune and shape the trees. When we are done, they look like real Christmas trees!

In the fall, we measure and tag the trees. Grandpa uses a wooden pole painted with different-colored rings. The pole shows how tall a tree is, so we know how much it will cost.

A tree as tall as the orange ring is four feet tall and gets an orange tag. Blue means five feet. A tree that is six feet gets a red tag. The tallest trees are marked with yellow tags and are seven feet and up. It takes more than fifteen years for a Christmas tree to grow that tall! It is no surprise that trees with yellow tags are the most expensive.

Grandpa closes the Tree Hut early on
Christmas Eve. I count the money while he
oils and hangs the saws until next year.

This is the day when aunts, uncles, and cousins come to Grandpa and Grandma's house for an old-time tree-trimming party.

In the backyard we decorate the blue spruce with strings of popcorn and cranberries, birdseed wreaths, and stars of suet. We stand at the window and watch the birds feast in the glow of our Christmas tree.

Virginia Pine
Colorado Blue Spruce
Scotch Pine
Fraser Fir

Norway Spruce
Balsam Fir
White Pine
Douglas Fir

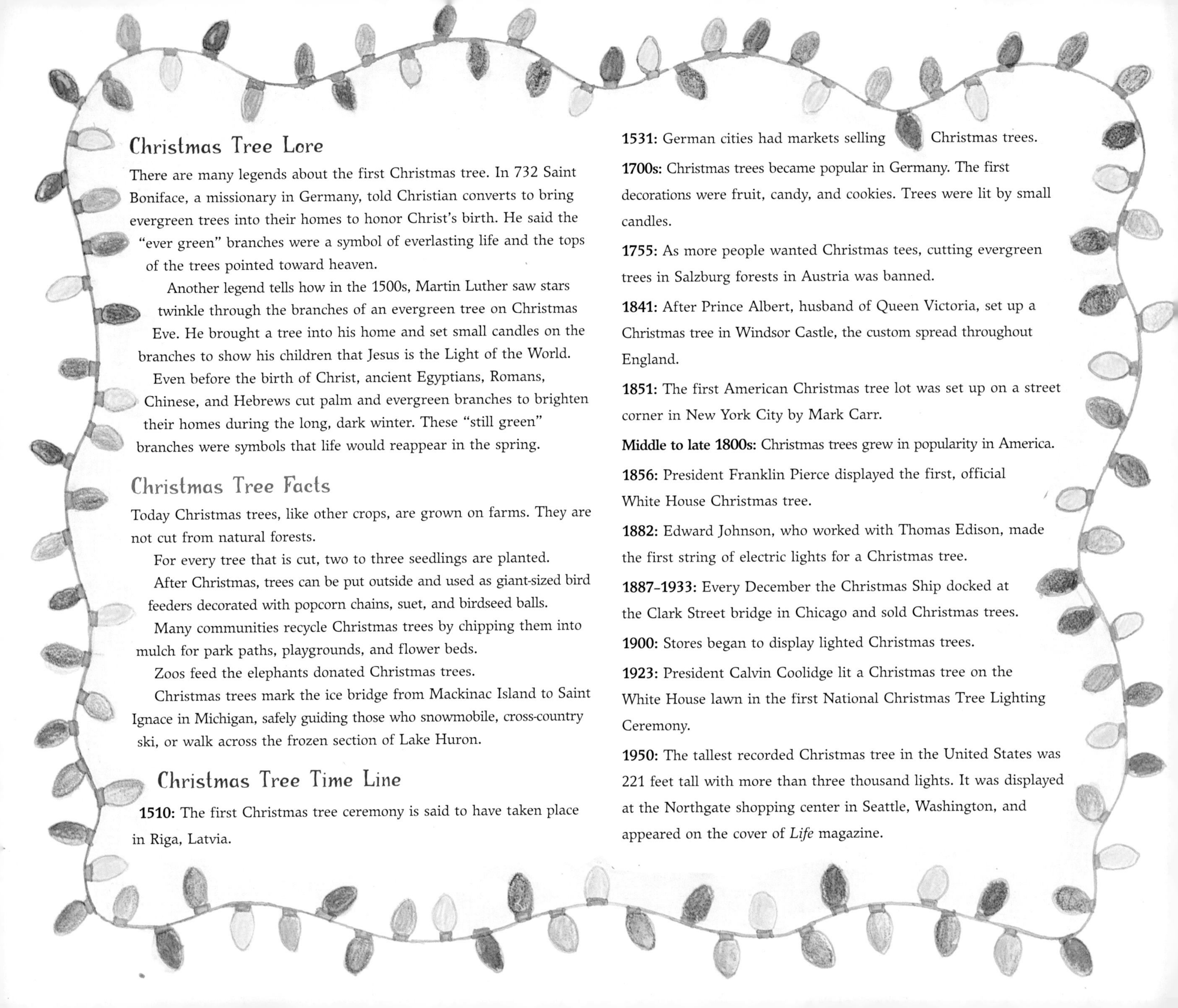

Christmas Tree Lore

There are many legends about the first Christmas tree. In 732 Saint Boniface, a missionary in Germany, told Christian converts to bring evergreen trees into their homes to honor Christ's birth. He said the "ever green" branches were a symbol of everlasting life and the tops of the trees pointed toward heaven.

Another legend tells how in the 1500s, Martin Luther saw stars twinkle through the branches of an evergreen tree on Christmas Eve. He brought a tree into his home and set small candles on the branches to show his children that Jesus is the Light of the World.

Even before the birth of Christ, ancient Egyptians, Romans, Chinese, and Hebrews cut palm and evergreen branches to brighten their homes during the long, dark winter. These "still green" branches were symbols that life would reappear in the spring.

Christmas Tree Facts

Today Christmas trees, like other crops, are grown on farms. They are not cut from natural forests.

For every tree that is cut, two to three seedlings are planted.

After Christmas, trees can be put outside and used as giant-sized bird feeders decorated with popcorn chains, suet, and birdseed balls.

Many communities recycle Christmas trees by chipping them into mulch for park paths, playgrounds, and flower beds.

Zoos feed the elephants donated Christmas trees.

Christmas trees mark the ice bridge from Mackinac Island to Saint Ignace in Michigan, safely guiding those who snowmobile, cross-country ski, or walk across the frozen section of Lake Huron.

Christmas Tree Time Line

1510: The first Christmas tree ceremony is said to have taken place in Riga, Latvia.

1531: German cities had markets selling Christmas trees.

1700s: Christmas trees became popular in Germany. The first decorations were fruit, candy, and cookies. Trees were lit by small candles.

1755: As more people wanted Christmas tees, cutting evergreen trees in Salzburg forests in Austria was banned.

1841: After Prince Albert, husband of Queen Victoria, set up a Christmas tree in Windsor Castle, the custom spread throughout England.

1851: The first American Christmas tree lot was set up on a street corner in New York City by Mark Carr.

Middle to late 1800s: Christmas trees grew in popularity in America.

1856: President Franklin Pierce displayed the first, official White House Christmas tree.

1882: Edward Johnson, who worked with Thomas Edison, made the first string of electric lights for a Christmas tree.

1887–1933: Every December the Christmas Ship docked at the Clark Street bridge in Chicago and sold Christmas trees.

1900: Stores began to display lighted Christmas trees.

1923: President Calvin Coolidge lit a Christmas tree on the White House lawn in the first National Christmas Tree Lighting Ceremony.

1950: The tallest recorded Christmas tree in the United States was 221 feet tall with more than three thousand lights. It was displayed at the Northgate shopping center in Seattle, Washington, and appeared on the cover of *Life* magazine.